The Dragon Who Couldn't Breathe Fire

A Book about Being Different

Educational Technologies Limited

A Child's First Library of Values

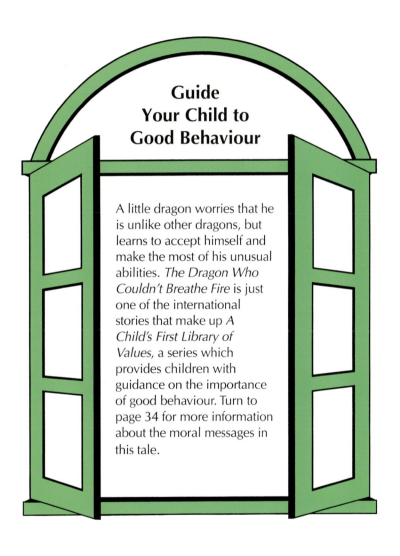

**Guide
Your Child to
Good Behaviour**

A little dragon worries that he is unlike other dragons, but learns to accept himself and make the most of his unusual abilities. *The Dragon Who Couldn't Breathe Fire* is just one of the international stories that make up *A Child's First Library of Values*, a series which provides children with guidance on the importance of good behaviour. Turn to page 34 for more information about the moral messages in this tale.

※ Everyone knows that dragons breathe fire.

The little green dragon in this story knows it too. But no matter how hard he tries, he just can't breathe out any fire. Not even a puff of smoke.

This makes the little dragon so unhappy that he decides to run away from home. He sets out into the woods, looking for someone who can teach him how to breathe fire.

※ know   ※ dragon   ※ breathe fire

✳ The little dragon walks until night falls and it gets dark.

"Now what shall I do?" he asks himself. "I'm tired and hungry and I can't walk any more."

✳ tired ✳ hungry ✳ wise

❋ Nearby, a wise old owl is sitting quietly on the branch of a tree.

"Try the house over there," he hoots, pointing in the direction of a tall house.

 In the house lives a witch and her three grey cats.

"Who's knocking on my door at this time of night?" she asks sleepily, yawning as she and the cats look out of the window.

"Sorry to disturb you," says the dragon, "but I've come a long way and I'm very tired. May I stay here for the night?"

The witch is a very kind and friendly witch. She makes the little dragon comfortable and gives him some hot soup and biscuits. Her cats bring him a hot-water bottle.

"Why are you out here all by yourself?" the witch asks him.

The dragon explains that he is looking for someone who can teach him to breathe fire.

"That's no problem!" says the witch. "My magic will have you breathing fire in no time. We'll start first thing in the morning."

* hot soup   * biscuit   * hot-water bottle

✳ pointed hat   ✳ mutter   ✳ mix

Next morning the witch puts on her pointed hat and takes out her book of magic spells.

"Let me see," she mutters to herself. "Breathing fire. . ."

The spiders watch as she mixes the ingredients together.
In the next room, the little dragon waits patiently. He is full of excitement at the thought of soon being able to breathe fire.

✳ ingredient   ✳ spider   ✳ wait

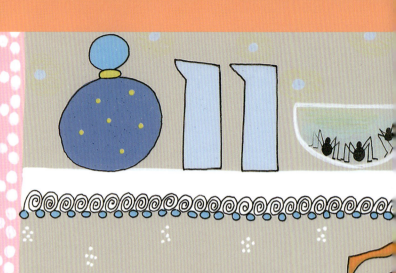

✳ "The spell is ready," announces the witch. "All you have to do is drink this magic potion."

The little dragon closes his eyes and swallows the potion. He thinks about fire.

The witch, the cats, the spiders and a frog in a jar all watch him carefully. They wait for something to happen.

"Hey, I feel warm all over," he says, getting excited.

"Now breathe out," says the witch.

✳ announce   ✳ drink

something   mouth   pretty

✳ Oh dear! Something is coming out of the dragon's mouth, but it isn't fire. He's breathing out hundreds of pretty butterflies.

"Whoops!" says the witch. "I must have used the wrong ingredients. Let's try again."

assure   chase

🌸 "I'll get it right this time," the witch assures them.

The butterflies flutter around and the cats chase after them.

Finally, the second magic potion is ready to drink. One of the cats pours it into the dragon's open mouth.

The little dragon gets ready to breathe fire.

🌸 second   🌸 pour

lots and lots of   colorful   fish

✳ Surprise! This time the little dragon breathes out lots and lots of colourful swimming fish.

The cats are delighted. They jump around catching the fish.

"Oh no!" says the witch, feeling embarrassed. "What's gone wrong? I'll try again."

✳ prepare ✳ third

The witch prepares another magic potion. "This time it can't go wrong," says the witch, and she holds out the third potion to the little dragon.

The cats watch excitedly. They are hoping for more fish. The dragon is hoping for fire. The witch is hoping the spell will work.

flower   smell   clap

Oh dear! This time the dragon breathes out lots of beautiful flowers. They smell nice too.

The witch claps her hands.

"What lovely flowers," she says cheerfully. "Aren't we clever? Flowers are much nicer than fire."

The dragon thinks about it for a while. It's fun to breathe out flowers instead of fire. Being like other dragons doesn't seem important any more.

Then the witch has an idea.

"Why don't we open a flower stall?" she suggests. "You can breathe out the flowers and I'll make beautiful bunches for sale."

suggest   flower stall   business

Soon the flower stall is ready for business. The cats have come to help sell the flowers. "Come and buy our wonderful flowers," they all call out.

help   buy

✳ The flower stall is a huge success.
People come from far and wide to buy the
colourful, sweet-smelling flowers.

   The little dragon's father and mother hear about
the famous flower stall and the flower-breathing
dragon, and they come to see for themselves.

✳ success   ✳ father   ✳ mother

☀ "Everyone loves your flowers," they tell him. "It doesn't matter whether you breathe fire, fish or flowers. We still love you. Why don't you come home again with us?"

The little dragon goes home with his parents, where he opens another flower stall.

He is happy knowing that he doesn't have to be the same as other dragons. He is special just the way he is.

Do you remember?

Can you answer these questions without looking back at the story?

1. Who gives the little dragon directions in the woods?
   a. a squirrel
   b. a cat
   c. the witch
   d. an owl

2. Whose house does the dragon find in the woods
   a. the woodcutters
   b. the witch
   c. a bear
   d. an old lady

3. How many grey cats does the witch live with?
   a. one
   b. two
   c. three
   d. four

4. What does the little dragon breathe out after the witch's first spell?
   a. butterflies
   b. flowers
   c. fish
   d. smoke

Do you know?

Look again at the story. Can you answer these questions?

1. Why does the little dragon feel so unhappy that he decides to run away from home?

_____

_____

2. Instead of running away, what else could the little dragon have done?

_____

_____

3. Imagine you are the little dragon, what would you like to breathe out instead of fire, and why?

_____

_____

4. Why do the parents want the little dragon to come home with them?

_____

_____

What can you see?

1. Look at pages 16 and 17. How many butterflies can you see?

There are _____ butterflies.

2. Look at pages 20 and 21. How many fish can you see?

There are _____ fish.

3. Look at pages 24 and 25, what can you see?
Why does the little dragon think it is not important to be like the other dragons anymore?

_____

_____

_____

Positive thinking

Write a sentence using each of these expressions. Start each sentence with 'It is good ...' and give a reason for your thoughts.

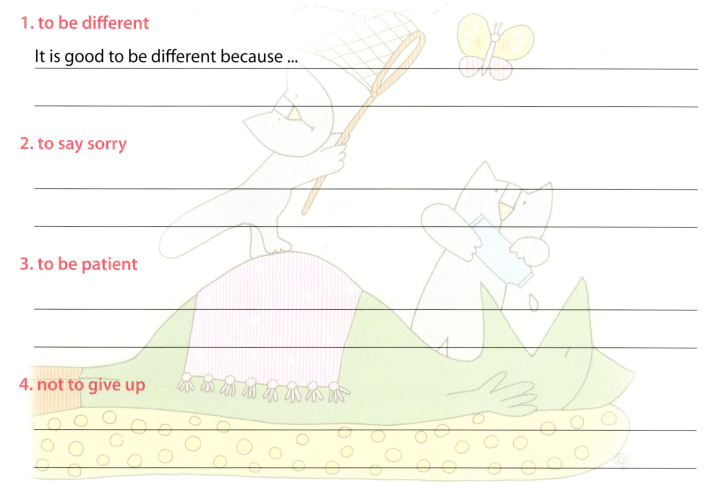

1. to be different

It is good to be different because ..._____

_____

2. to say sorry

_____

_____

3. to be patient

_____

_____

4. not to give up

_____

Find the way

Can you help the dragon find his way through the woods to the witch's house?

Being different

Write a few words about each member of your family, and highlight the different qualities that each person has. The box below contains some words which you can use.

1. My father is __is____Yo,_uynger___ and _____.

2. My mother is _____, _____ and _____.

3. My brother is _____, _____ and _____.

4. My sister is _____, _____ and _____.

positive
tidy
funny
kind
quiet

Everyone is good at something. Write the names of two of your best friends and describe what they are good at:

1. _____ is good at _____, _____ and _____.

2. _____ is good at _____, _____ and _____.

3. I am good at _____, _____ and _____.

Let's make a 'Thank You' card

Imagine you are the little dragon. Make a 'Thank You' card to send to the witch to thank her for her help. For the front of the card, draw a picture of yourself at home with your parents. Show the witch how happy you are.

Now write the words for the inside of the card. Remember to include all the polite features of a 'Thank You' letter.

Useful expressions
- Dear ...
- I hope you are well
- Thank you so much for your kind help
- I am very grateful for your help
- I will always remember your kind help
- Give my love to the cats
- Thinking of you
- Yours sincerely,
- Best wishes,

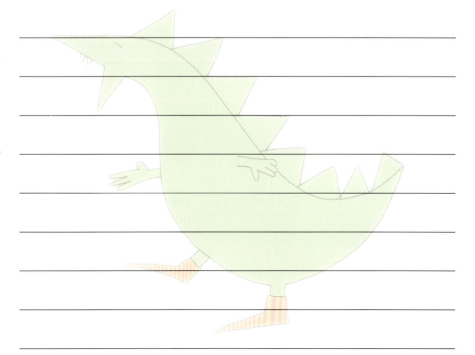

What the story tells us. . .

- **Being different.** The dragon in the story wants to be able to breathe fire so that he will be like other dragons. In the same way, we often want to be like other people, because we are afraid of being different. But we should realize that it is alright to be different from other people. In fact, every one of us is a different individual and this makes us all special in our own way. We should learn to accept ourselves as we are and not worry about being different from others. In the story, the dragon realizes that his inability to breathe fire is not important. He discovers a way to make the most of his ability to breathe flowers instead of fire, and he soon realizes that self-acceptance is the key to happiness.

- **Asking for help.** If we get lost, or are on our own in a strange place, we shouldn't be afraid to ask a reliable person for help. In the story, the little dragon finds himself in the woods at night. He knows he needs to find somewhere to stay the night, so he takes the wise owl's advice and asks for help at a nearby house.

- **Sorry to disturb you.** When we disturb someone late at night or at an inconvenient time, it is polite to say sorry, just as, in the story, the little dragon apologizes to the witch for disturbing her.

- **Being patient.** The dragon in the story waits patiently for the witch to finish making each magic potion. He knows that he won't gain anything by being impatient, even though he is very excited. Being impatient doesn't help things to happen more quickly – it just annoys people who are trying to help us. Sometimes we get excited about new things and we don't want to have to wait, but we should remember the little dragon and try to follow his example.

- **Not giving up.** If something doesn't work right the first time, we should keep trying and not give up. In the story, the witch doesn't get her spells right, but she keeps trying until she finds one that she and the dragon are happy with.

- **Being positive.** Sometimes things don't work out quite as we have planned. But we should try to see the best in any situation and look at it in a positive way. When the dragon discovers that he can breathe flowers instead of fire, the witch thinks of a positive way to use this unique ability and the dragon finds that he likes breathing flowers after all.

- **Not running away.** Running away from home doesn't solve any problems. If we have a problem or are worried about something, it is much better to talk to our parents about it, rather than running away. The little dragon is so unhappy about his inability to breathe fire that he runs away from home. When his parents find him at the end of the story, they explain that it isn't important whether or not he breathes out fire like most dragons. Instead, they love him just the way he is and are proud of his unusual ability to breathe flowers. People who love us will always be proud of us, whether or not we are different or unusual.

A Child's First Library of Values
The Dragon Who Couldn't Breathe Fire

Authorized English-language edition published by:
Educational Technologies Limited
A member of the Marshall Cavendish publishing group

First published 1997. New Edition 2017.
Printed in China.

Original story and illustration by Nicoletta Costa.
Nicoletta Costa was born in Italy in 1953. She graduated from Venice University and is a storybook writer and illustrator in Europe and the United States.

Original Japanese-language edition published by:
Gakken Co. Ltd., Tokyo, Japan
© Nicoletta Costa/Fumiko Takeshita and Gakken Co. Ltd. 1992

ISBN-10: 0-7835-1304-6
ISBN-13: 978-0-7835-1304-1

 www.ETLlearning.com